THE LOVE TRIALS

BOOK ONE

J.S. COOPER & HELEN COOPER

THE LOVE TRIALS

BOOK ONE

PROLOGUE

"I want to make you mine." His voice was low and hoarse, and I shivered in the darkness.

I felt the light touch of the feather being guided along my naked body, and I knew that I needed to become his as well. I wanted to become his. I had to become his. I whimpered slightly as I felt something cold touch my skin.

"I'm going to make you forget your own name." His voice became louder as he guided the feather farther down.

"Please," I whispered as I felt what must have been an ice cube grazing my nipple. "Oh." I trembled as he ran the melting ice cube across my breasts. I could feel the residue of water on my skin.

"Please what, Nancy?"

"Please," I moaned in high anticipation.

It was then that I felt his warm breath on my breasts as he eagerly licked up the water, sucking gently on my nipples as if he were enjoying every last drop of water. I felt the tip of the feather moving between my legs as he teased me. I gasped as his finger accidentally grazed me, and I cried out when his finger touched me again. That time hadn't been an accident.

"I'm going to leave you now," he said.

I heard him step away from me, and I froze. My hands were still handcuffed to the bed and I couldn't move.

"What do you mean?" I cried out, my whole body aching for him.

"You're not ready yet."

"I am," I whispered, embarrassed to admit it.

"No, no you're not." His fingers trailed between my legs again and he played with my wetness. "Your body is ready, but you are not."

There was silence in the room as he continued playing with me. I clenched my legs to trap his fingers. I needed him to know how badly I wanted him.

"That's not enough, Nancy." His voice was deep, and I could imagine the look on his face. "I will not make you mine until every fiber in your body has to have me."

"I do want you," I whispered.

"Not enough. I will not take you until you are screaming out my name and begging me. I won't take you—not until there is no other thought in your mind but me inside you. I won't take you—not until I know I possess every inch of you." He leaned down and pressed his lips gently against mine, and then he walked away.

CHAPTER ONE

The invitation, when it arrived, wasn't entirely unexpected. I knew as soon as I saw the crisp, white linen envelope with the neat, black calligraphy handwriting that my time had come. I picked it up quickly and surreptitiously and then ran to my room. There was no way I wanted my nosy little brother, Harry, asking me what it was. Or even worse, my dad, Brandon. Shit, if he knew what was in the envelope, all hell would break loose. He'd probably lock me up and throw away the key. I giggled as I locked my bedroom door. There was no way in hell that I could let anyone know what was in the envelope. No way at all.

I was a normal eighteen-year-old girl—if you ignored the fact that I'd recently found out that my sister was my mother and the man I'd grown up hating was my father. I know, I know. I already sound like the first guest on the Jerry Springer Show. I could practically hear the people in the audience whispering, "That's Nancy Hastings, crazy old Nancy Hastings." And they'd all stare at me in awe. Only they wouldn't know the most scandalous part of my life at all. That was yet to come.

I opened the envelope slowly and carefully, taking my time before I stared at the card that was going to change my life. I pulled the crisp, cream-white card out of the envelope and read it quickly. My heart beat fast as I perused the short and simple note.

"Nancy Hastings, you've been accepted to the Lovers' Academy. We expect you to arrive in one week."

I swallowed hard as I realized this was it. This was the moment I'd been waiting for. For the last two years, I'd been in love with a man named Hunter. He didn't know that I existed. Or at least he pretended that he didn't know. He was at least five years older than I was. I didn't know his exact age. All I knew was that he was the most handsome man I'd ever seen and that, when he smiled at me, I felt like birds were chirping in my ears. I knew, in my head, that he was the one for me. I mean, if one can feel as strongly as I did for him, well, then it had to be true love.

I always blamed our not getting together on the fact that he had been a teacher at my school, but I wasn't a student now and he was no longer my teacher. At least not in the academic sense. I was hoping he'd become my teacher in other ways. In ways of the mind and body. In ways of the soul. I imagined him to be my soul mate. I'd had so many dreams of him when I was in school that sometimes I barely knew what was reality and what was make-believe. To be fair, it was all make-believe and I was just obsessed with him. However, my dreams were about to become reality and I couldn't wait.

***

The day I was supposed to arrive at the academy approached slowly. And as it grew closer, my resolve grew weaker and weaker. I wasn't sure how I was going to leave my new family to go to a sex school. If my dad ever found out, I knew he would kill me. Especially after everything that had gone down at the private club he'd started with his best friend, my uncle Greyson.

As the day to leave grew closer, I decided that I was no longer going to attend. Yes, I had a crush on Hunter. Yes, I'd sent off an application hoping to be accepted, but I'd never really thought it through properly. I knew that I couldn't just go. I tried to pretend that I was happy about my decision, but I wasn't. I wanted to be there with every fiber of my being. In fact, my suitcase was still packed and ready to go. Only, I wasn't sure if it was the right move.

Then another letter arrived.

Nancy Hastings, you have a date with your destiny. The lovers' academy awaits you and so do I.

Mr. X

I swallowed hard as I realized that they wanted me at the academy as much as I wanted to be there. Had Hunter sent me the letter? I shivered as I grew excited. Hunter wanted me there as badly as I wanted to be there. He had to be the one who'd sent the letter. I knew then and there that I had to go. No matter how scared I was about the situation. Or my dad finding out.

"Brandon," I called out as I walked into the living room. I still found it hard to call him Dad.

"Yes, dear," he called back with Harry in his arms, squirming and giggling as he was swung around upside down.

"Does Katie know you're treating Harry like a monkey?" I raised an eyebrow and laughed at the two of them.

"Nancy," Harry giggled. "You look funny." Then he screamed as Brandon swung him around the room.

"Thanks, Harry. I love to be complimented. You're going to be a hit with the ladies when you get older." I grinned down at him, and Brandon laughed and put Harry on his feet on the ground.

"The earth is spinning." Harry collapsed on the floor and giggled some more.

I shook my head at my five-year-old brother and went over to give him a hug. I was going to miss him while I was at the academy.

"Hey, dad." I looked over at Brandon, my heart thudding. "One of the colleges I wanted to go and see is having an orientation this weekend. I was thinking I could go and then go and see some friends next week." I bit my lower lip as I lied, praying that my face wasn't turning red.

"This weekend?" I could hear the frown in his voice.

"Yeah, why?"

"I thought Katie wanted you to—"

"I wanted Nancy to do what?" Katie walked into the room, and Harry jumped up and ran towards her.

"Mommy!" he screamed and ran to her arms.

"Nancy wants to go and look at a college this weekend."

"Oh." She looked at me. "I thought you could come with Meg and me to look at bridesmaid dresses."

"Oh, can we go when I get back? I'm really interested in this school." I smiled at her weakly, hating having to lie.

"I guess." She gave me a small smile. "Meg will be disappointed."

"I'll see her soon." I leaned down and played with Harry's hair.

If there were anyone I would feel guilty about lying to, it would be Meg. She was one of my closest friends and confidantes. She was the first person I had really trusted in a long time. I wanted to tell her the truth, but I knew she would tell Katie what I was up to. And I knew if she told Katie, then Katie would tell Brandon and that would be it. There was no way that he would let me go. I'd only been in his life for a short while, but he was making up for lost time by being an extremely overprotective dad.

"Do you want me and Meg to come with you?" Katie looked at me consideringly.

"No!" I blurted out loudly and then paused before trying to explain away my resistance to them coming. "I mean, it's so not cool to have your parents at the orientation."

"Can I come, Nancy?" Harry looked up at me. I pulled him up and he gave me a hug.

"Next time." I kissed his cheek and held him close to me. "You can come next time."

"Ewww, kissing!" He pulled away from me and we all laughed.

CHAPTER TWO

On Friday evening, I took a train from Penn Street Station with my backpack, $500 in cash, and a new American Express credit card. I stared at the Google directions I'd found for the address on the invitation. This was it. I was finally on my way.

I slowly opened my backpack and looked at the invitation again. I wondered if Hunter had sent it to me. Had he been excited that I had applied? Had he even recognized my name? I bit my lower lip as I realized that I had no idea if Hunter even knew I existed outside of the classroom. What if he hadn't even seen my application? I sighed as I realized that I had no real clue as to what awaited me at the lovers' academy. In fact, I didn't really know what the lovers' academy was all about. I had an idea, but I had no real clue.

It had been my mother's ex-boyfriend Frank who had tracked down Hunter for me. He was the one who had told me where Hunter worked. I had found a mysterious website and sent off an application saying why I wanted to be a student at the academy. I knew there was some element of sex to the academy, but I wasn't sure.

Another worry crossed my mind. What if he didn't recognize me? I looked at my reflection in the window and stared at my long, dark-brown hair and brown, worried eyes. I wasn't sure how memorable I was. I sighed as I realized that I really had no clue if Hunter had been the man known as Mr. X or not.

"Going somewhere fun?" the middle-aged man sitting across from me asked me in a friendly tone.

"Yes, thanks." I nodded and stuffed the invitation back into my bag.

I noticed a man a few seats away giving me a hard look. I stared back at him for a few seconds, wondering what his problem was. He looked like he was rich, with his navy-blue pinstriped suit and shiny shoes. His face was classically handsome, with his bright, shrewd, green eyes and jet-black hair. He gave me another dismissive look and looked away from me. I frowned to myself. What was his problem?

"So where are you off to?" the man across from me asked.

"To visit a friend," I lied smoothly.

I studied the man in front of me. He looked like he was in his sixties or seventies, old enough to be my grandfather. He had lines in his face, and I wasn't altogether sure if his smile was genuine or not.

"That's nice," he continued. "I'm going to visit my son."

"Oh, very nice," I answered back, wondering if my nice demeanor meant I was going to have to talk to this man for the whole journey. I sighed as I realized that I wouldn't have much time to make a game plan for what I was going to do when I arrived at the academy.

"I'll let you get back to your thoughts," the man said kindly, and my face flushed as he laughed at my surprised expression.

"I didn't mean to be rude." I gave him an awkward smile and looked away from him.

I saw the other man staring at me again. He had a look of derision on his face, and part of me wanted to go over and ask him what his issue was with me. I sat back, closed my eyes, and tried to think of Hunter instead of the man staring at me. I opened my eyes again after a few seconds and looked over to see what the arrogant-looking man was doing, but he wasn't there. I jumped up and smiled at the man across from me.

"Do you mind watching my bag? I just need to go to the bathroom."

"Sure, my dear." He smiled. "You can trust me."

"Thanks. I'll be right back."

I made my way through the car and stopped dead when I realized the arrogant man was waiting by the restrooms. I was about to go back to my seat when I saw him look my way and then turn back around again. *Jerk!* I thought to myself and continued walking to the restroom. I stopped behind him and stared at the 'occupied' sign on the door, praying for it to turn to 'vacant' soon.

The arrogant man turned to look at me and nodded his acknowledgment. His eyes were a darker green than I had thought, and he was even more handsome close up. He had the beginnings of stubble on his face, and I could see the traces of red wine on his lips. I waited for him to say something to me, but he kept quiet. I felt quite peeved at his silence. I felt like he was judging me even though he didn't even know me. He looked to be about twenty-five. I tried to ignore the fact that I was wildly attracted to him. There was something so mysterious in his gaze. I looked away from him and sighed. I felt slightly guilty that I was so attracted to him when I was on my way to meet up with Hunter.

Ding, ding, ding. Some bells went off in the train, and suddenly, all the lights went off. I was caught unawares and fell forward into the man. I fell against his back and held on to his arms to steady myself in the dark. He felt warm and hard. His arms were muscular and his back was stiff. My breasts crushed against him, and my breathing deepened as I realized just how close I was to him. I could smell the deep musk of his cologne as I straightened myself up and stood back.

"Sorry about that," I whispered, feeling embarrassed.

"It's not a problem." He grabbed my arms and brought me towards him. "Are you okay?"

"I'm fine, thanks." I nodded as he stared into my eyes.

"Good." The pressure of his fingers on my arms increased, and he moved towards me slightly.

I took a step back and felt the wall against my back. He took another step towards me and I felt his body pressed up against mine as he looked down into my eyes. I stared up at his lips and wondered if he was going to kiss me. I licked my lips in anticipation. I couldn't help it. There was some sort of wild animal attraction between us. I'd never felt a buzz like this before. Not even with Hunter. I wanted him to kiss me. I wanted to know what it felt like to have a kiss with a stranger on a train. I closed my eyes and waited to feel his lips on mine. I could feel his hardness against my stomach, and I moaned slightly.

"Next time, try and be more careful," he whispered in my ear and let go of me. I slowly opened my eyes, and he stepped away from me.

"I said I'm sorry," I muttered, feeling dazed.

"Sometimes, sorry isn't enough." He frowned at me and then muttered something under his breath. "I'm going back to my seat." He looked at me and then walked back to his chair.

I stood there, unsure of what had just happened. Why hadn't he kissed me? I sighed in frustration as the bathroom door opened and an apologetic-looking lady walked out. I walked in, crouched above the seat, and wondered what the deal with the guy was. Why had he been such a jerk? I had been so sure that he was going to kiss me. I walked back to my chair and made sure that I didn't acknowledge the man at all. I wasn't going to waste any more time thinking about him. He was nothing to me. I kept repeating that in my head over and over again. *He means nothing to me. He means nothing to me.*

Without knowing it, I fell asleep. My dreams were vibrant and full of handcuffs and dark corners.

"I think this is your stop." The man across from me nudged my shoulder and woke me.

I blinked up at him in confusion, the mysterious man's face still in my mind. "Huh?"

"This is Cadestown." He nodded at the sign on the tracks.

"Oh." I jumped up and grabbed my backpack. "How did you know I was coming to Cadestown?"

"I saw your ticket." He smiled. "You better hurry before they pull off."

"Yeah, thanks." I smiled at him again before running and jumping off the train. I heard the conductor ring the bell and then watched as the train left the station.

"That was a close one, wasn't it?" a dry voice whispered in my ear, and I jumped.

"Argh!" I shouted out in surprise and turned around to face the handsome man from the train.

His eyes studied my face intently, and then he frowned. "You shouldn't fall asleep on the train like that."

"Excuse me." I pulled my backpack onto my back.

"It's not safe."

"It's none of your business." I looked back at him and squared my shoulders. "Maybe you should just worry about yourself."

"I was just trying to give you some advice."

"I don't need your advice." I took a step away from him.

His eyes narrowed as I moved away from him, and a small smile crossed his face. "Alrighty then." He nodded. "Goodbye." And with that, he walked away.

I stood there watching him walking away and felt a slight twinge of regret. I wasn't sure why, but the man had unnerved me. I bit down on my lip and stood there for a few minutes. I was starting to feel anxious again. I wasn't sure if I was doing the right thing, and I hated that I had lied to my family. I hated it more than ever.

I pulled the invitation back out of my backpack and stared at it again. It was so classy, so elegant, so full of promise. And if I had been invited because of Hunter, well, I couldn't just walk away from that. Not after all these years of crushing on him. I took a deep breath. I truly believed that Hunter was my soul mate, and this was the only way to find out if he felt the same way.

I walked to the front of the train station and looked around for a cab. I sighed as I realized that Cadestown was a far cry from New York City. There was no line of cabs waiting outside the train station. I stood there feeling sorry for myself when I noticed two other girls walking towards me.

A cute blonde smiled at me. "Hi."

"Hi." I nodded back at her, taken aback at her friendliness.

"You going to the academy?"

"Yes." I blushed. "How did you know?"

"I figured." She giggled. "There aren't many of us out here, and well, you look lost."

"Yeah." I sighed. "How are we supposed to get there?"

"I think a car is going to come and pick us up."

"Oh, cool."

"I'm Amber by the way."

"Nancy." I smiled at her.

"This is Shannon. She's shy." Amber nodded towards her friend.

"Hi, Shannon."

"Hi," Shannon whispered back at me, her eyes looking scared.

"Don't mind her." Amber laughed. "Shannon didn't want to come, but I told her that that there was no way I was coming by myself."

"Oh. That was nice of her." I tried smiling at Shannon again, but she looked down at the ground. I felt a bit rude talking about her in third person when she was standing there with us, but I wasn't sure what to say.

"She's a virgin," Amber spoke in hushed tones.

"Oh?"

"Not for long though." Amber started laughing, and I watched Shannon blush.

"Why do you say that?"

"Why?" Amber looked at me in confusion. "We're going to the lovers' academy. The place that teaches you to be the best lover possible."

"Best lover possible?" My words were low as my body froze. "So we have sex?"

"We don't just have sex. We're taught to be the best lovers we can be." She grinned.

"Oh?" I felt like my eyes were popping out. "Best lovers we can be?" I repeated slowly.

"You don't know?" Amber's face looked shocked, and then she had a wicked gleam in her eyes. "No way. How do you not know? You have to apply to come here."

"I applied, but I didn't really know exactly what I was applying for." I wrinkled my nose. "I thought it was just a camp to teach us about sex and stuff, maybe some tricks. I didn't know we'd be expected to have sex." I shuddered.

"Well, you do what you want." Amber laughed. "They can't make you have sex. That's rape. However, we're all assigned an instructor. The instructor is there to teach you to become a seductress, a woman of the world, a woman who can get any man she wants to do anything she wants him to do."

"Through sex?"

"Haven't you heard of the power of the pussy?"

"Amber." Shannon shook her head, and I looked at her in surprise. "Sorry about that. She's known to be vulgar."

"You can talk." I laughed, and she laughed as well.

"I guess your shock brought me out of my shell." She shook her shoulders. "I don't know how I let her convince me to come."

"Because you want hot sex." Amber grinned, and Shannon groaned.

"No, we came because you want hot sex."

"I came because I want hot sex to get me a powerful man on Wall Street. I want to live in a penthouse on Fifth Avenue and I want a summer home in the Hamptons." Amber's eyes shone. "And sex will get me that."

"Why did you come then, Shannon?" I asked her curiously.

"I came to support Amber." She shrugged and then grinned. "And I guess I came because it sounded exciting. And well, I'm still a virgin and don't want to be. Guys don't really like me that much." She shrugged. "Maybe because of the way I look?" She gave me an awkward smile and sighed as she played with her long, brown hair.

I studied her face and noticed that she was slightly overweight. Not obese or anything, but it was noticeable that she had a few extra pounds. She had a really pretty face and a sweet, genuine smile. Her body was curvy, but she was wearing an ill-fitting outfit. I had a feeling that, if she were wearing a different outfit, she would definitely stand out a lot more.

"So what about you, Nancy? Why did you apply to the lovers' academy if you didn't come to learn how to be an excellent lover?"

"Ugh," I groaned, not wanting to admit my reasons. I knew that they would sound childish and obsessive when spoken out loud, and as much as I liked the two of them already, I wasn't sure if I trusted them enough to tell them.

"Come on, Nancy." Shannon smiled at me. "Tell us."

"Okay," I sighed. "This is going to sound crazy, but when I was in high school, I met this guy and I fell in love with him. His name is Hunter, and he's handsome and funny and smart. And well, I just kind of fell under his spell. When I graduated, I had a family friend figure out where he went and found out he worked here, so I decided to try and join the academy so I could see him again. And hope we fall in love." I took a deep breath. "Sorry. I sound crazy, don't I?"

"No." Shannon smiled. "That sounds sweet and romantic."

"What didn't you just date him when you were in school?" Amber frowned. "Wouldn't it have been easier to make a move then?"

"He was my teacher," I mumbled and looked down.

"Oh." Amber's eyes lit up. "Spicy. I like it."

"Amber loves crazy." Shannon shook her head.

"That's right. The crazier the better." Amber grinned.

Shannon smiled at me. "You'll fit right in with us."

"Aren't we all crazy?" I looked at them and made a face, and we all just stared at each other for a few minutes.

It was then that a limousine pulled up in front of us. We all watched as an elderly man got out of the front door. He was dressed in a black suit, and he walked up to us with a somber expression.

"Ms. Hastings, Ms. Blake, and Ms. Lucas, I presume?" He bowed in front of us, and we all stood there gaping at him. He looked back up at us and gave us a small smile. "I'm Henry, the chauffeur at the Lovers' Academy."

"Nice to meet you, Henry." I gave him a small smile, and he turned to look at me.

"Thank you. Are you girls ready?" He grabbed our bags and carried them to the trunk of his car. He hurried back to us and opened the door for us. "Enjoy the ride, ladies."

***

The lovers' academy was nothing like the private club I had been in a couple of months before. Where the private club had been large and creepy, the academy looked comfortable and stately, like a nice, comfy country home. Henry dropped us off outside the house, and a lady with kind eyes welcomed us into the house.

"I suppose you girls are hungry and thirsty?" she asked us as she ushered us in.

"I wouldn't say no to a beer." Amber grinned, and the lady smiled.

"I don't think so, Ms. Blake. We don't serve alcohol to minors." The lady smiled at her kindly. "But I can get you a root beer."

"What the fuck?" Amber frowned as the lady left the room. "Can you believe that?"

"I guess they don't want to get into trouble?" I shrugged.

"We came here to have sex and they care about a little alcohol?" She shook her head and frowned.

I jumped up out of my chair and walked to the door. "I'm going to look for a restroom. I'll be right back." I walked through the door and looked around the foyer with interest before hurrying down the corridor and opening a door. "Oh sorry," I muttered as I realized that there was someone in the room. "Oh." My jaw dropped and my face went white as the man turned around. It was the mean guy from the train.

"Hello." His eyes looked at me with a hint of a smile, but he didn't look surprised to see me.

"Hi," I answered him, not smiling. Why oh why did he have to be at the academy?

He took a step towards me. "What's your name?"

"Nancy," I whispered.

"What?" His lips curled up as he studied my timid expression.

I spoke up louder and glared at him, annoyed by his imperious expression. "My name is Nancy."

"That's more like it." His eyes turned a brilliant sparkling green, and he smirked at me. "I like a girl with a bit of fire in her."

"Excuse me?" I stared at him in shock as he reached over and ran his fingers down my neck and to my collarbone.

"I said I like a girl with a bit of spark in her. There's nothing like a bit of screaming to know you're doing the job right."

"What job?" I frowned at him, swallowing hard. I could still feel my skin burning where he had touched me.

He turned away from me then without answering and wrote something down on a pad. It was when he looked back up at me with a dark expression that I realized I hadn't gotten the wrong impression of him on the train. This guy was trouble. Once again, I felt like I was in over my head.

"You may go now Nancy." He nodded his head. "Unless you'd like to stay the night."

"No." I shook my head vehemently, and he laughed.

"I can't wait for the moment when you beg me to stay," he whispered, not smiling, and I stared at his handsome face as if frozen.

"When I beg you to stay?"

"No, when you beg me to stay the night with you." He smirked cockily.

"Not going to happen." I took a step back.

"There will come a time when you will not be able to get enough of me." He smiled at me and took a step towards me.

"I doubt that." I shivered as I stared at his fingers. "You're not a teacher here, are you?" I crossed my fingers behind my back. *Please don't be a teacher here.* I touched my collarbone unconsciously, still feeling the burn.

He smiled again. "There will come a time when you'll be remembering more than my fingers, Nancy," he leaned in and whispered in my ear. I could feel the tip of his tongue lightly caressing my inner ear, and I swallowed hard. "And no, I'm not a teacher here. I'm so much more than that."

His breath tickled me, and I knew then that this was going to be the experience of my life. And I wasn't quite sure if it was going to be the experience I had come for.

CHAPTER THREE

"Where have you been?" Amber looked up as I reentered the room.

"I told you. I needed the restroom." I avoided her gaze and sat down. I didn't want to tell her about my encounter with the man. I didn't even know his name. Or why he was here.

"The lady was looking for you." Amber made a face. "Her name's Louise."

"Oh, do you think I should go and find her?" I jumped back up again.

"Nah." Amber sipped her drink. "She's coming back with the teachers. I guess we're the only three in this class."

"Oh wow." I looked surprised, though I really had no idea what that meant.

"Are you excited, Nancy?" Shannon asked me. "Do you think Hunter is going to be your teacher?"

"I sure hope so." I nodded eagerly at her, but my mind fell to the guy I'd just been talking to.

He oozed sex. But dangerous sex. Kinky sex. He screamed of wild nights with whips and chains. I shivered as I thought about all the dirty things I'd read about in erotic romance books. He looked like the type of guy into pleasure and pain, unlike my Hunter. Hunter was one hundred percent pleasure.

"Aren't you freaked out though?" Amber spoke up, and I looked at her in confusion.

"Freaked out about what?"

"Aren't you freaked out that he fucks women for money?" She raised an eyebrow at me. "He's like a male ho."

"I don't know what he does," I responded, but my heart ached at her words. I hadn't thought about that before. Did Hunter sleep with every girl who came to the academy?

"Yeah." Shannon gave Amber a look. "None of us knows exactly what goes in here."

"I can't wait to find out though." Amber grinned and fluffed her short, blond hair. "I have to get a guy with a big cock who knows how to go all night looonng." She winked at me and then laughed. "I'm not shocking you, am I, Nancy?" She licked her lips and laughed again. "I'm not a virgin. I like sex, and I want to learn every trick that I can."

"If you're so good, why are you here?"

"I want to learn all the secrets." She shrugged. "The lovers' academy will teach me that."

"I see." I sat back in my chair and closed my eyes.

I could feel my phone vibrating in my backpack. I knew it had to be Katie or Brandon calling me, asking me if I'd made it to campus safely. I'd have to call them back soon and make up some excuse about a mixer.

I heard the door open, but I didn't open my eyes right away. I think I was too overwhelmed.

"Girls, the teachers are here," Louise said.

I slowly opened my eyes, and my heart started thumping when I saw Hunter. He was here. My Hunter was here. I was about to jump up and run to him, but then I realized that would be awkward. I gave him a huge smile, but he didn't seem to notice because his eyes left mine and continued looking at the other girls.

"Shannon, your teacher is going to be Hunter. He's going to take you to your suite and explain how everything works."

My heart dropped as I watched Shannon standing up. She gave me an awkward smile and walked towards him. He looked so handsome standing there, with his golden-blond hair. I tried to make eye contact with him again, but he didn't even look at me again before he left the room.

"Amber, you're going to be with Keenan," the lady continued, and Amber jumped up eagerly.

"See you later, sweets." She grinned at me and practically ran to the front of the room.

It was then that I realized that there was no one left in the room aside from Louise and myself.

"So, Nancy. It's just you and me." She smiled at me. "I'm going to escort you to your room. Your teacher, Ryan, missed his train this evening. He'll be joining you tomorrow."

"Oh okay." I frowned.

"What's wrong?"

"I thought I'd be with Hunter?" I spoke slowly and tried to ignore the disappointment in my stomach.

Hunter had acted like he didn't even know me. How could he not know me? Was I wrong? Had he not been the one to accept me into the academy?

"Are you ready, Nancy?" She stepped forward, and I realized that I hadn't heard what she'd said.

"Yes, sorry. I was just daydreaming." I smiled at her weakly and stood up. "Let's go see my room."

I followed her into the foyer and then up a flight of stairs. She paused at the top of the stairs and then pulled out her ringing phone.

"Hello?" she answered, and her eyes lit up. "Hold on." She placed her hand over the phone and looked at me. "Nancy, your room is the last door on the right. Make yourself at home.

We'll see you tomorrow morning." And then she walked back down the stairs.

I sighed as I made my way down the corridor. I was already regretting coming to the academy.

I walked into the bedroom feeling tense. I didn't know what was going to happen tonight. I had seen Hunter once and he hadn't even given me a second glance. I couldn't believe it. I was in shock, and I felt hurt and angry at myself. How could I have been such an idiot?

"Sit down," said a deep voice as soon as I walked through the door.

I looked around, but I could only see the silhouette of the man in the dark.

"Huh?" I answered dumbly.

"I said sit down."

"Hunter?" I asked hopefully.

"Nancy, have a seat on the bed." The voice was dry. "And no, this isn't Hunter."

"Oh." I paused and my heart started beating. "Who are you then?"

"I'm your teacher."

"Teacher?" I frowned. Hadn't Louise just said he wasn't arriving until tomorrow?

"That's why you came to the academy, yes?" He chuckled. "You came to learn."

"I thought Hunter would be my teacher," I whispered.

"You thought wrong." The voice was no longer humorous.

I reached the edge of the bed and sat down. "What are you going to do?"

"What do you want me to do?" He chuckled again, and I froze.

I finally recognized the voice. It was the man from the train, the man I'd met when I'd first arrived. The arrogant asshole who'd been so rude to me.

"I know who you are." I gasped. "You're not a teacher."

"I am tonight." He stood up and walked over to the bed. He turned on a lamp at the side of the bed and then turned towards me. He looked down at me with a sardonic smile, his eyes dark and shadowed.

"You can't just become a teacher." I stared up at him, trying to ignore the feelings that were building up in my stomach.

"I can do whatever I want."

"But..." I stuttered and watched as he loosened his tie.

"As the owner, I can do what I want." He ran his hands through his hair, and I stared at a gold ring on his pinky finger.

"What are you going to do?" I questioned him again, wondering if I should run out of the room.

"I'm not going to touch you."

"Oh." I looked down, feeling confused and slightly disappointed.

"I'm going to blindfold you and handcuff you." His voice was rough. "And I'm going to let you see what anticipation feels like."

"What?" My voice rose, and I looked at him with wide eyes. "How?"

"You'll have to wait and see."

I swallowed hard as he spoke. His voice had become silky, and I felt like he was already seducing me.

"But you're not going to touch me?"

"Not with my hands." He grinned at me and leaned towards me. "Not unless you beg me," he whispered in my ear before pulling back and staring into my eyes. His blue eyes mocked me as he stared at me with a smug smile. "Now, take off your clothes. Leave your underwear on though." He brought a finger up to my cheek and ran it down to my trembling lips. "If you beg me, I'll take those off as well."

"I'm not going to beg you to do anything."

"We'll see." He grinned. "What are you waiting for?"

"I'm not going to take off my clothes." I jumped off the bed and walked towards the door. "Are you crazy?"

"Isn't that why you came here, Nancy?" His voice cut through the room. "Or are you chickening out already?"

"I don't know you," I whispered and stared at him as he threw his tie onto the ground. My brain was screaming at me. What the fuck was going on here?

"Do you want to get to know me?" He started undoing his shirt.

"Not particularly." I shook my head.

"I think you want me." He took a step towards me.

"You're a creep." I licked my lips as he continued walking towards me.

"You were breathing heavily on the train." His voice was soft. "I could see your lips trembling as you stood next to me. I could feel your body heat rising. I could feel your nipples against my back hardening."

"I don't know what you're talking about." I shook my head, but I couldn't move.

"When you fell against me." He stopped in front of me. This time his shirt was all the way open. "When you fell against me, you held on to me tight. You held on to me longer than you had to."

"I was disoriented."

"You were horny."

"No, I wasn't." I shook my head.

"That's what we do here, Nancy." He stared into my eyes as he whispered against my lips.

"What are you talking about?"

"We make you own up to the truth about your feelings." He smiled as he gently licked my bottom lip.

"I am being honest."

"No, you're not." He cocked his head and smiled at me gently. "I can see in your eyes that you're attracted to me. I can tell from the way your nostrils are flaring that you're a bit angry, a bit confused, and a bit turned on. I can tell from the flush on your face that I'm making you hot. I can tell from the fact that you're still standing here that you're intrigued. You want to know what's going to happen next."

"No," I whispered, still unable to move. My eyes widened as he pulled his shirt off and threw it on the floor. "What are you doing?"

His chest had a sprinkling of dark hair, and he was as muscular and built as I'd thought.

"I'm getting ready." He grinned at me like a wolf before dinner.

"Ready for what?"

"Ready to take you to bed."

"You're not taking me anywhere," I gasped out.

"No?" He moved towards me again, and I took a step back.

"I don't even know your name."

"That's all you need?" His eyes sparkled and he laughed as my face turned red.

"No, no. I'm just saying that I don't know your name. Not that I would sleep with you if I knew your name."

"It's Jaxon."

"Jaxon?" I repeated.

"Yes." He grinned and stepped forward again. "Are you ready now?"

"No." I took another step back and hit the wall again.

He moved towards me and placed his hands against the wall on either side of me, pressing himself against me. I could feel my heart racing as my body once again welcomed his warmth.

"Now?" he whispered.

"No." I pushed him away from me. "What are you doing?"

"So you do have some fire in you then?" He stepped back, picked his shirt up off the floor, and buttoned it up.

"Huh?" I looked at him in confusion. "What's going on here?"

"I wanted to test you." His smile faded and he looked at me seriously. "We don't allow women who can't speak up for themselves to enter the academy."

"So this was all a test?" I frowned, suddenly feeling deflated.

"Yes." He nodded. "Or did you hope it was something else?" He paused and looked at me for a second. "Can I ask you something, Nancy?"

"Yes."

"Why did you apply to join the academy?"

"It sounded interesting." I shrugged.

"Do you know what we do here?"

"Of course." I nodded even though I still wasn't one hundred percent sure.

"Do you find me attractive?"

I bit my lip and stared at him for a few seconds before answering. "Yes," I answered honestly. I knew that he could tell that I was and I didn't want to lie—not after what he had said earlier.

"Do you want to touch me?"

"No." I shook my head.

"Do you want me to touch you?"

I bit down on my lip and looked on the ground. My body had jumped at his words, but rationally, I didn't know why.

"Nancy, answer me."

"I don't know." I shrugged.

"Because you feel conflicted and confused." He nodded. "That's what you're feeling. You just met me. You don't really like me, but your body wants me."

I stared at him in surprise. Was I that transparent?

"Are you hungry?" he asked, changing the subject, and I was thankful for it.

I was uncomfortable with his line of questioning. My body was madly attracted to him, yet I wasn't here to meet someone like him. He seemed too dark, too much like a tortured soul. I could still remember the way he'd stared at me on the train. Why had he looked so curious and angry as he'd stared at me?

"I'm fine." I shook my head and walked towards the bed.

"I thought you might like to see your two new friends and their teachers."

"Oh, they'll be there?" I asked casually and turned around to face him again.

"Yes, they'll be there."

"I suppose I can grab a bite." I looked down at the ground.

This was my opportunity to speak to Hunter. Maybe he'd been playing coy before. Maybe this would give us the opportunity to talk. Maybe he'd admit to having gotten me accepted into the academy.

"I'll see you downstairs." He nodded and then abruptly left the room.

I watched as he walked out, and I stood there thinking. Something wasn't right. I knew from previous experience that when something felt off, it usually was.

I hurried to the bed, sat down on the mattress, and pulled out my phone. I had four missed calls. Two from my dad and two from Meg. I quickly called Meg back and prayed that she would answer the phone.

"Nancy, where are you?" she whispered into the phone, and my heart stopped. Oh shit. What did they know?

"Why?" I whispered back.

Meg was my best friend. She was also best friends with Katie, who was my dad's fiancée and Harry's mom. I had met Meg while we had both been working at a private club. We'd been roommates, and we'd bonded over the secrets of the club. It was because of my time at the club that I'd found out that Brandon was really my father and that my grandparents had raised me as theirs.

"I know you didn't go to an orientation." She sounded worried. "You would have told me about it. What's going on?"

The phone was silent while she waited for me to answer. "Do you remember I told you about a guy I liked?"

"Do you mean Hunter?"

"You remember his name?"

"I remember the diary I read quite vividly. You should think about becoming a writer, you know."

"Oh yes." I cringed as I remembered that Meg had read the diary I'd left for her to help her figure out the clues of the private club.

"So you're with him?"

"Yes and no." I sighed. "I came to this place to be with him, but I'm not sure if he likes me or if he's playing hot and cold."

"Oh, Nancy." She sounded surprised. "I don't know what to say. I should tell Katie and Brandon, but I know what it's like to fall in love with someone." She sighed. "Promise me you're going to take care of yourself and come home quickly."

"I promise. So, Meg." I started feeling a bit embarrassed. "What do I do? Do I let him know I like him?"

"Hmm. What has he said to you so far?"

"Well, he—" I stopped talking as Jaxon walked into the room. "Hey, what are you doing? I thought I told you to knock before you came in here?"

"Who are you on the phone with?" He walked over to me, frowning.

"My friend."

"Your friend who?"

"None of your business."

"Can I speak to Noneofyourbusiness? I'd like to tell them they have an interesting name." His eyes flashed at me as he raised an eyebrow at me.

I could hear Meg laughing on the other side of the phone.

"Is that him?" She hissed.

"No," I said loudly, feeling annoyed but trying to answer both of them at the same time.

"Are you ready for dinner?" Jaxon looked me over, and I shivered at his long, intense gaze as his eyes wandered the length of my body.

"I thought we were meeting downstairs?"

"I changed my mind." The corners of his lips turned up, but he wasn't smiling.

"I'm not ready."

"Well get off of the phone and get ready."

"I will." I rolled my eyes at him. "Just leave the room and I'll change."

"I don't need to leave the room for you to change."

"Wow. He sounds like a bit of an ass," Meg whispered. "Is that Hunter then? Are you sure you want him?"

"No, I'd be crazy to want *him*," I said loudly, and his eyes narrowed.

"Are you talking about me?" He took another step towards me, and I looked up into his thoughtful, green eyes. "Are you telling your friends how attracted you are to me? How you want to rip my clothes off?"

"You wish."

"I wouldn't say I wish." He chortled. "But I definitely wouldn't say no."

"You seem so unprofessional."

"I didn't know there was a professional side to a lovers' academy." He smirked, and I heard Meg gasp.

"What did he just say, Nancy?" Her voice rose, and I knew that if she heard much more, she would no longer be encouraging me to stay.

"Hey, I gotta go. I'll talk to you soon." I hung up the phone quickly and frowned at Jaxon. "Please don't just walk into my room again. It's very annoying."

"I own the building. I can do what I want."

"I have an expectation of privacy whether or not you own the building."

"Expectation of privacy? Did someone go to law school and not tell me?"

"I'm starting college in the fall."

"Are you now?" He cocked his head and looked at me for a few seconds.

I stared back at him and tried to ignore the fact that I was quite enjoying our back-and-forth. He made me feel alive inside, like I had a new vitality, a new way to express myself and my voice. I'd been so quiet and kept to myself the last couple of years. I'd never really wanted to make waves or speak out. I'd always been the quiet one, the docile one, but now? Now I was enjoying being the feisty one.

"Let's go eat." I walked to the door and looked back at him. He was waiting for me to join him. I could see the surprise in his eyes and the rise of something akin to respect.

"It's been less than a day and you're already getting a backbone." He smiled to himself as we walked to the door. "That's what I like to see."

***

"Nancy!" Amber jumped up and ran over to me as soon as Jaxon and I entered the large dining hall. "There you are." She gave me a quick hug and whispered in my ear, "You lucky bitch. Your teacher is so hot."

"He's okay." I turned around and looked at Jaxon as he sat down and talked to a guy I hadn't seen before.

I didn't bother telling Amber that Jaxon wasn't my teacher. There were about seven other girls in the room and everyone was talking excitedly. When Jaxon looked up as he was talking and caught me staring at him, our eyes connected for a few brief seconds before he looked away. I felt flustered and annoyed. Yet again, he'd given me an odd look. No smile, no recognition in his eyes. It was starting to get annoying.

"Are you okay that Shannon's with Hunter?" Amber asked me loudly and covered her mouth with a quick giggle. "Oops," she said and smiled.

I looked around the room and saw that Shannon and Hunter were at the end of the table, and both were just sitting there, looking bored. Something in my heart lit up when I saw their expressions. Hunter was just as upset as I was. He was mad that he was with Shannon and not with me. I was confident of that fact. Why else would he be looking so miserable?

"Nancy?" Amber looked at me. "Are you okay?"

"I'm fine." I grinned back at her. "In fact, I'm more than fine." I nodded and noted the surprised and disappointed look in her eyes. It was then that I realized that Amber was both friend and foe. "How are you liking your guy?"

'He's fine." She shrugged, and her eyes fell back to Jaxon. "But he's nothing like that hot piece of meat." She slowly licked her lips. "Now that's a man who could teach me how to fuck."

"Amber!" I scolded her, feeling irritated.

"What?" She laughed. "It's not like you want him. You're going after teacher boy over there?" She nodded to Hunter. "Me? Well, I'm after a man. A man who can make me forget my own name."

"Uh huh." I rolled my eyes.

"You won't mind if I make a play for him, will you?" She continued staring at him. "I wonder how big he is."

"Big?" I repeated, not thinking, and then froze. "Amber," I said again, my face flushing.

"Don't tell me you haven't thought about it!" She laughed. "I like them big, but not too big. I can't swallow too big, and the pounding you get from an oversized cock just isn't the same as one you get from a nice, medium-to-big cock. Though it can't be too thin. Thin, no matter how long, is a deal breaker." She looked back at me then and grinned. "Don't you think?"

"I've never thought about it before." I made a face at her.

She was putting images in my mind. Images of cocks. Images of Jaxon's cock. I felt him looking at me then, and I looked back at him, unblinking. Now all I could think about was how big he was. What he looked like down there. I trembled as I realized that my thoughts were completely dirty. My mind had started wondering what it would feel like to taste him. I shook my shoulders and took a deep breath.

"Get it together, Nancy. You're here for Hunter," I mumbled to myself.

"What?" Amber leaned towards me and frowned. "What did you say?"

"Nothing." I smiled weakly back at her. "I'm just hungry and ready to eat."

"I bet you are." She winked at me and walked back to the table. "I'll talk to you later."

"Okay." I watched her sit back down and just stood there for a few moments.

I didn't know if I should sit down or if I should wait for Jaxon. I looked over at Hunter again to see if he was going to make eye contact with me and then felt a tap on my shoulder.

"So you've made a new friend already?" Jaxon's voice was deep and dry, and I reluctantly turned around to look at him. I was still slightly embarrassed that I'd been thinking about his cock.

"Sorry, what?" I spoke, feeling flushed. Being so close to him again was making me feel disoriented. I watched as his eyes laughed at me, and he reached over and wiped something off my cheek.

"I didn't know you'd made a new friend so quickly."

"Oh, Amber? I met her and Shannon at the train station."

"Oh, so you were nice to someone at the train station?" His lips curled up, and I knew he was laughing at me.

"You weren't exactly a pleasure," I retorted back at him, and this time, he laughed out loud.

"Shall we eat?"

"That's why we're here," I snapped back and looked over at Hunter. From what I could tell, he still hadn't looked at me. "Hi, Shannon?" I called out across the room.

Both Shannon and Hunter looked up at me. Shannon gave me an awkward smile, and Hunter's eyes surveyed me with a cursory glance. And then he smiled and nodded at me. I grinned back at him, and I was about to walk over and say something to him when Jaxon grabbed me around the waist.

"Let's sit down." He pulled me towards the table.

"Hey, don't just grab me!" I pushed his hands off of me. "Also, I wanted to sit on the other side."

"There are no free chairs."

"I can pull one up." I glared at him.

"One?"

"I only need one." I smiled sweetly at him.

"You're a fool, Nancy." He shook his head at me and pulled out a chair for me.

"Whatever." I glared at him and tried not to stare at his lips. I wondered what they would feel like against mine.

I shivered as I remembered the feel of his muscular body against mine. He'd be a forceful lover, I was sure of that. He'd totally try and dominate me. I blushed at the thought and then chided myself. *You want a gentle, sweet lover to be your first, Nancy. Not some brute,* I mentally lectured myself.

"What would you like to eat?" He leaned forward, and my breath caught as I stared into his deep, vivid green eyes.

"I don't know," I mumbled.

"Bye, Nancy," Shannon called out to me as she exited the room.

Hunter was in front of her, and he didn't even look back and acknowledge me. I didn't understand what was going on. Why was he pretending that he didn't remember me? I'd been in two of his classes. And if he wasn't the one who had gotten me to the academy and sent me the note telling me that he was waiting for me, then who had?

"Don't look so disappointed, Nancy. It doesn't suit you," Jaxon's voice whispered in my ear.

"I'm not disappointed about anything."

"Liar." His expression changed, and he sat back. "I'll order for us both."

***

I was too disappointed to eat much during dinner. Though that didn't seem to disappoint Jaxon, as he didn't attempt to talk to me. The walk back to the room was silent as well. I felt deflated and confused inside. I didn't even ask Jaxon why he was walking back to the room with me. I was glad for the company, even if it was him. Odd, arrogant, mysterious Jaxon.

"I can help you," he said as we reached my room.

"Help me with what?"

"I think you know." His eyes bored into mine.

"How are you going to help me?" I stared at his face for a few seconds. "And why would you want to help me?"

"If you want to learn how to catch the man of your dreams, I can help you."

"I want the man of my dreams to catch me," I responded right away.

There was only so much I was willing to do. I wasn't sure I could go through a whole seduction routine and get rejected and not feel completely depressed.

"What makes you want Hunter anyways?" he asked me curiously.

"What do you mean?" I frowned, my heart beating rapidly.

"Look, I know you think that you're good at keeping your emotions in and hiding your feelings, but you're not. It's pretty obvious you have a thing for Hunter. I just want to know why."

"You wouldn't understand." I looked away from him, my face red.

"Did you come here for him?"

"Yes."

"Then someone did their homework right, didn't they?" He laughed, but there was no humor in his eyes. "As your teacher, I can help you."

"I don't want you to be my teacher."

"I'm the best," he responded lightly and then stared at my lips for a few seconds.

His gaze fell to my breasts, and I could feel my nipples tingling. I shifted uncomfortably as I realized that my panties were growing wet. His intensity was starting to turn me on.

He smiled as I ran my hands through my hair. Then he grabbed my hand and swiftly moved me into the room and towards the bed.

"Wait! What are you doing?" I gasped as we say down on the edge of the bed.

"I'm showing you anticipation." He smiled. "The anticipation of sex, hot sex, can be even more thrilling and even more panty wetting than sex itself."

"I thought you were supposed to teach me how to seduce a man. Not show me how you can seduce me."

"You can't seduce a man if you don't know what it is to be seduced." He reached over and played with my hair, twirling it in his fingers like silk. "You can't make love with your eyes if you don't know what it looks or feels like. You can't promise a million orgasms with one flick of your tongue across your lips if you've never experienced the thrill of climbing Mount Everest."

"I don't like climbing."

"Then you're lucky that I do. And I don't mind carrying you on my back."

I stared at him breathlessly. My legs were tingling as they rubbed up next to his on the bed. I swallowed hard as he spoke to me. His words were like words floating in front of my face. I could hear them. I could almost see them. Yet I didn't know what he was saying. Or rather, maybe I didn't want to know. He was like a wild, crazy lightning storm. Exciting to watch, but I was scared to get too close.

"Can I be your teacher, Nancy?" He reached out and grabbed my hand. "There's something about you that I like. There's something about you that makes me want to make this experience perfect for you."

"Are you in the habit of teaching?" I asked softly.

"No. You'd be my first." His index finger ran circles around my palm.

"I see."

"Do you like how this feels?" His finger continued caressing my palm, and I nodded. "Good." He dropped my hand. "Attraction is key in every coupling."

"Coupling?" I sighed and thought of Hunter.

"I can help you get any man you want, Nancy." His voice was soft, and I looked up at him in surprise. Was he a mind reader?

"Why do you care? Why are you here?" I studied his face. I could see the hints of lust in his eyes, but there was also something else, an emotion I couldn't define.

"I'm here because I want everyone to get what they came for when they applied to the academy." He pulled away from me. "I can see that you have a lot to learn."

"What does that mean?"

"You wear your emotions on your face." He looked at me and studied my face. "I can see that you still have a slight dislike of me, but you're curious and you're attracted to me. You want to explore what I have to offer, but you also feel guilty." He reached over and touched my slightly trembling lips with his fingertips. "You can be attracted to me, Nancy. I'm not the big, bad wolf." He slipped his finger into my mouth, and my eyes widened at the salty taste. "This isn't bad. This is pure. This is unadulterated lust."

His eyes clouded over as I sucked on his finger, my lips taking over my mind. "Maybe your heart wants Hunter, but your body wants me."

He pulled his finger out of my mouth and pushed me down on the bed. His hands grabbed the sides of my face and he stared into my eyes for a few seconds before his lips came crashing down on mine. They were everything I'd imagined them to be. His lips crushed against mine in an all-consuming manner. They were firm yet soft at the same time. They were moist and seeking.

His tongue entered my mouth slowly, as if he were taking his time, allowing me to experience every part of this kiss with every part of my body. My fingers reached up to his hair, and his tresses felt silky and soft to the touch. I opened my mouth slightly, and he groaned against me as our tongues played with each other. All of my senses were on fire. I'd never been kissed like this before.

Then I felt his hands move away from my face and down my body. His fingers lightly grazed my breasts, and I froze slightly. His fingers kept moving down, and then he leaned up and smiled down at me.

"So, Nancy, what do you say? Would you like me to be your teacher?"

"Yes." I nodded in a daze, and he smiled.

"Goodnight, Nancy." He jumped up and walked to the door. "I'll see you in the morning.

CHAPTER FOUR

"Today is fantasy day." Jaxon walked into my bedroom, and I quickly pulled the sheets up.

"There's such a thing as knocking before you walk in the door." I glared at him as I watched him approaching me. Was it possible that he looked even more handsome in the light of the day?

"What's the fun in that?" He grinned and walked over to my bed. "Are you naked?"

"No, of course not."

"What are you wearing?"

"Pajamas," I responded indignantly as he pulled the sheets away from me. "What are you doing?"

"I wanted to check what you were wearing to bed."

"I already told you."

"Those aren't sexy." He looked at me and sighed. "That's a baggy t-shirt and what appears to be sweatpants."

"So?"

"So, you're never going to have a man salivating over you wearing that."

"What should I be wearing then?"

"Nothing." He grinned. "Or a cute teddy."

"Teddy?" My mind imagined a large teddy bear covering me.

"Also known as negligee." He sighed.

"Oh, I don't have one." I made a face. "Plus, it's just me sleeping here."

"Unless you always want it to be only you, I think you should heed my advice."

"Fine," I huffed.

"Good girl. Now, as I was saying, today is fantasy day."

"What's fantasy day?" I sighed.

"We play out one of your fantasies."

"What do you mean?"

"I mean what I said," His fingers ran down my neck. "We're going to role-play."

"Why?"

"So I can see just how much help you need." He laughed. "Once I see how you act out your biggest fantasy, I can see what areas you need to improve in."

"You're not expecting sex, are you?" My eyes narrowed.

"No, Nancy. That only happens when you want it." He smiled at me seductively and then reached over and cupped my breast.

"What are you doing?" I gasped as his fingers pinched my nipple.

"I'm playing with you." He smiled gently. "I wanted to see how horny you were this morning." He then leaned forward and kissed me softly. "So what's your fantasy?" he whispered against my lips.

"I don't have one." I pushed him away from me, my face flushed.

"I don't believe you." He smirked. "Tell me."

"Why don't you tell me yours?"

"My fantasy would be to fuck on a stage in front of a crowd of people so everyone could see just how well I get my woman off."

"Oh." I stared at him in surprise. "Why haven't you done that yet?"

"Haven't met the right woman." He shrugged. "It's your turn now."

"I don't know."

"You must have at least one fantasy."

"I suppose I've always wondered what it would be like to be a stripper. I had a friend in school who used to tell me stories, and I always wondered why she found it so exciting." I bit my lower lip.

"So you want to be a slutty stripper?" His lips twitched.

"No." I blushed. "I was just saying that—"

"Today, you're going to be a stripper for me." He jumped up. "I want to see how comfortable you are with your sexuality."

"I'm comfortable," I muttered.

"Last night, you seemed tense."

"I wasn't expecting you to do that." I blushed.

"It felt good though, didn't it?" He smiled at me, and I didn't answer.

"Are you done?" I stared at him. "It's rude of you to just barge in my room."

"Oh, Nancy. You have a lot to learn." He laughed.

"What's your normal job here, Jaxon? Why are you so intent on helping me?" I frowned. "You didn't seem like you were particularly interested in others when we were on the train yesterday."

"Do you know what I was thinking when we were on the train yesterday?" he whispered and sat on the bed next to me.

"What? How to look like an arrogant asshole?"

"No, Nancy." He laughed. "I was thinking, 'I wonder what that girl would say if I asked her to go into the bathroom with me.'"

"Bathroom?" I frowned.

"I wanted to fuck you hard and fast. I wanted to see your eyes widen as you felt me enter you. I wanted you to bite down on my lips so hard that they bled as you came so hard and fast that you couldn't control yourself."

"Oh." I shivered. "You didn't even know me."

"That didn't matter." His eyes sparkled. "You need to understand, Nancy. Lust and sex know no boundaries. What your body wants cannot be controlled."

"I'm not looking for sex."

"What are you looking for?"

"Love." I looked down, slightly embarrassed. "I'm looking for love."

"What about passion."

"It has its place as well."

"Passion makes for the best kind of love." He leaned towards me and whispered against my lips, "You want a man to need you so badly that he'd do anything to be with you. You want a man who will do anything for one kiss from your lips. You want a man who will walk over hot coals for one touch of your fingers. You want a man who would give his life for one night with you.

Isn't that what you want, Nancy?" His eyes stared into mine, unblinking.

I nodded slowly, my heart beating fast.

"When you have that power, then you can make any man fall in love with you."

"I-I…" I bit down on my lower lip. "Love isn't sex."

"That's where you women fool yourselves. Men aren't looking for love. They are looking for the woman who intrigues them, who puts them under their spell, who makes them think illicit thoughts, who captures their mind and body. Once you have them in your web, then you will have love."

"Aren't you scared?" I whispered.

"Scared of what?" His eyes looked at me in confusion.

"Aren't you scared that I'll catch you in my web?" I smiled slightly and stretched.

His eyes fell to my breasts, and he looked back at me with a twinkle in his eye. "You can't catch the master in a web." He reached over and ran a finger down my cheek. "No one can catch the master."

***

I showered quickly and tried to dismiss thoughts of Jaxon from my brain. He was entirely too confusing and arrogant for me. I wasn't sure who he thought he was. Master, my ass. He was so full of himself. I quickly pulled on my clothes and carefully applied my makeup. I wanted to look good if Hunter saw me. At least that was what I told myself. I hurried down the stairs and saw Jaxon waiting for me in the foyer.

"Ready?" He reached his hand out to me as I walked up to him, but I ignored it.

"I guess. Where are we going?"
"On a drive."

"A drive where?" I frowned.

"You'll see. It's a secret."

"I'm confused." I sighed as we walked out of the door. "Is this part of the course?"

"Every teacher teaches differently."

"I don't really understand the point of the academy."

"What do you want to understand?"

"Why are you bringing girls here for free to teach them to seduce men? What do you get from it?"

"The pleasure of knowing that I made a difference." He responded, and I shook my head.

"Makes no sense. What pleasure?" I frowned. "How do you make money?"

"I have benefactors."

"What benefactors?"

"So many questions, Nancy. Can't we just enjoy the day?"

"I don't get it. What does a drive have to do with a fantasy or me seducing Hunter?"

"The drive is taking us to a place that will answer some of your questions."

"Oh my God, you're not taking me to a strip club, are you?"

"No," he laughed. "Though that would be a good idea."

"So where are we going?"

"Wait and see."

I changed the subject. "Who goes through the applications?"

"Why?" He opened the car door for me.

I jumped into the passenger's seat of his black convertible BMW and sat back in the plush leather seat. "Curious."

"We have a committee that goes through each application."

"Oh, okay." I looked away from him. So maybe Hunter hadn't been the reason why I'd been accepted. "Where are we going?"

"Patience, grasshopper."

"Yes, master," I replied sarcastically and laughed.

"I like the way you're thinking."

"So, Jaxon, tell me more about you."

"What do you want to know?"

"Age, where you went to school, why you think you're such hot stuff—that sort of thing."

"I'm twenty-five. Went to Harvard undergrad, Wharton for business school." He shrugged. "I'm boring."

"Why are you so guarded?" I looked at his profile, talking my thoughts out loud.

"I'm not."

"On the train, I smiled at you. If you'd been so interested in me, why didn't you smile back? You gave me a nasty look."

"I didn't give you a nasty look. That's your imagination. And I wasn't interested in you. I had a thought about what it would be like to fuck you. That was all."

"Wow, nice. That makes me like you more than I did before." I rolled my eyes at him, and he laughed.

"I like that you don't hide back your thoughts."

"Why would I?"

"I don't know. You just seemed more reserved on the train."

"I guess." I leaned back into the seat.

He'd been correct in his thoughts. I normally wasn't so outspoken. I wasn't sure what it was about him that made me just forget all my inhibitions.

We didn't speak for the rest of the ride. Instead, I looked at my surroundings. They were really quite picturesque. It was exciting to be surrounded by so much green and nature after living in cities all my life.

We pulled off a tiny dirt road and I looked at Jaxon with narrowed eyes.

"Where are we going?" I frowned.

"You'll see." He gave me a quick glance and smiled.

"Uhm, no. I barely know you and you're taking me to the middle of nowhere. Tell me where we're going."

"You should have thought about that before you got in the car with me." He smirked. "I warned you that you need to be more careful."

"Whatever."

"Whatever? Ha. Aren't you mouthy?" He smiled to himself. "Not that that's a bad thing. I like a woman who likes to use her mouth."

I ignored him and stared in front of me, anxious to see where we were going. Then I saw a huge, grey concrete building with a small, black door.

"Where are we?" I leaned forward, my heart racing.

I closed my eyes for a second. I knew he'd looked like a psycho on the train. Why had I gone with him so easily? This was it. He was going to kill me.

"You'll see." He laughed. "You can open your eyes, Nancy." He pulled the car for a stop, and I jumped out of the car.

"Tell me or I'm not going anywhere." I looked towards the ground, saw a rock, and picked it up. "I'll hit you. Don't test me."

"Oh, Nancy." His lips twitched. "This is a store."

"What sort of store is this?"

"It's a sex store."

"Sex store?" I looked back at the building.

"There's a lot going on in there. Don't worry." He took a step towards me. "I'm not going to take you to the rooms."

"The rooms?" I frowned and took a step back.

"The rooms where we get to try out all the different equipment."

"Oh." I frowned again and stared at him carefully. I no longer felt as worried. I felt excited. I wanted to slap myself.

"I want you to choose an outfit."

"Outfit?"

"For tonight."

"Tonight?"

"When you become Nancy the stripper."

"Nancy the stripper?" I made a face. "One, that sounds boring, and two, I'm not becoming a stripper."

"That's your fantasy, right?"

"It's not anything I want to be in real life." I shook my head.

"But you'd like to see what it feels like?" He raised an eyebrow. "You'd like to see how one dance can turn on a man?"

"I don't know." I bit down on my lip, imagining myself dancing for Jaxon.

"The first lesson you need to learn about seduction is that you have to be sure. You have to be confident. You have to own your sexuality. You have to be proud of what you want. You cannot be embarrassed. You cannot lie to yourself. You have to own it. Your sole purpose is to entice. Doubt in your mind will confuse your intended target."

"I don't want a target. I want a man. A man who—"

"This isn't the time for the lovey-dovey shit. That comes later—if you do your work well."

"You mean if I wiggle my ass fast enough?" I shot back, and he laughed.

"You get it." He grinned. "Only, you want a man to get hard as soon as he sees you, not when you start wiggling on him. Once you can get a man hard from one sight of you, then you know you've got it."

"What sort of outfit am I looking for?" I sighed.

He was right. I wanted a man to have to have me. I wanted Hunter to take one look at me and rush over to me. I wanted Jaxon to push me down on the bed and have his wicked way with me. I wanted his eyes to be green with lust and desire. I froze as I realized that my thoughts had switched from Hunter to Jaxon in a heartbeat.

"Whatever you want." He started walking towards the building. "Don't be nervous, Nancy."

"I'm not nervous," I lied and followed him through the doors.

My eyes widened as I walked through the door. It was completely unexpected. The place was bright and full of color.

There was a row of doors to the right with blacked-out windows, and to the left were aisles and aisles of items that I gathered were sex toys.

"Go to the back and make a left. You'll see the outfits there."

"You're not coming?"

"No. Surprise me." He grinned. "I'm going to check out the toys."

"What for?"

"You'll see." He winked at me and walked away.

"I'm not going to sleep with you," I whispered behind him and took a deep breath.

This was not what I had signed up for. Then I laughed at the irony of my thoughts. This was exactly what I had signed up for. I walked to the back of the room and took a left. There were racks and racks of outfits. I walked directly back, and my mouth dropped as I realized just how little material there was in most of the outfits. There were dresses so short they wouldn't cover my ass, crocheted tops that would show everything, beautiful silky pieces that were so sheer they would show every imperfection. Leather pieces that were so tight they'd hug every inch of me. Crotchless panties. Tops with no material where the breasts would be. I gasped as I looked at all the outfits. There was no way that I could wear any of these pieces. I moved on to the next rack.

This contained dress-up pieces. I saw a schoolgirl's outfit, a cheerleading outfit, a nurse's outfit, and a clown's outfit. I burst out laughing. Who would wear a clown's outfit to seduce someone? I stepped back and thought for a moment. I needed an outfit that was sexy but something I'd still be comfortable in. I knew there was no way in hell I was wearing a piece that had my breasts hanging out or my ass showing.

I wanted to surprise Jaxon though. I could tell that he didn't expect much from me. I knew that he assumed I'd get the least sexy outfit. And every fiber in my body wanted me to get the long nightgown I saw at the end of the rack. But I wanted him to be shocked when he saw me. I wanted his eyes to widen in surprise and lust. I wanted to put him off-kilter. I wanted to show him he didn't know me as well as he thought I did.

Yeah, I'd come with the hopes of being with Hunter, but I was no longer the innocent schoolgirl who'd daydreamed about her teacher. A lot had happened to me since then. I was no longer a silly little girl. I was a woman. I was a woman who was ready to win her sexuality. I was a woman who was intrigued by Jaxon.

There was an unmistakable attraction between us, and I was drawn to him like a moth to a flame. There were secrets in his eyes. There was something to his story. There was a man behind the mask. A part of me wanted to unravel his secrets. I wanted to unravel him. I just didn't know why I was so drawn to him. Or maybe it was just the lust. I couldn't deny that my body craved his touch, no matter how light and subtle.

I looked back at the outfits and pulled out a dress. It was black and sheer with small straps. It would probably fall just under my ass, and I knew it would show everything. I'd go braless, but I'd wear some panties.

I walked over to the row of panties. All were thongs. Some were edible. Some were crotchless. A couple had a lock and a key. I grabbed a plain black thong and was about to walk away when my hand involuntarily grabbed another pair—a crotchless pair this time. These was for my night with Hunter, I told myself. I'd allow Jaxon to teach me all he knew, but I wouldn't sleep with him. I'd save myself for Hunter.

I flushed as I thought about seducing Hunter. Would he like it? I closed my eyes to picture his face, but all I could think about was Jaxon. His dark, brooding face filled my mind. I could see his green eyes staring at me, with his perfect white teeth grinning as clearly as if he were standing right in front of me.

I quickly opened my eyes and rubbed my forehead. I was worried that I was getting in over my head. I wasn't even able to concentrate properly anymore. My mind was playing games on me and my body was reacting in ways I'd never experienced before. I hurried to the front of the store to pay for the items before Jaxon found me.

"There you are." I heard his voice behind me as I finished paying.

"Hey." I smiled at him as I grabbed my bag. My body flushed as I thought about wearing the outfit for him.

"You paid?" He frowned.

"Yes. I wanted it to be a surprise."

"You shouldn't have paid."

"Why not? I wanted to pay. It's my stuff."

"You're too hardheaded. I wanted to pay." He sighed. "What did you get?"

"You'll see later."

"Hmm." He looked like he wanted to say something more, but he didn't. "Okay. Let me pay for my stuff."

"What's that?" I glanced at the items in his hand.

"You'll see." He smiled.

"Tonight?"

"Unlikely." He shook his head.

"Oh." I was slightly disappointed.

"Unless you want to?" He picked up a box from the counter and showed it to me.

"What's that?" I stared at it wondering what it was. It looked like a slightly larger silver bullet.

He grinned. "Something to pleasure yourself with."

"What?"

"You have to be able to give yourself pleasure to know what pleasure you want from a man."

"Okay?"

"Plus, there's nothing that turns on a man more than watching a woman pleasuring herself. It makes a man determined to give her more pleasure than she can give herself."

"Okay," I said again.

"I want to watch you play with yourself, Nancy," he whispered in my ear. "I want to see your fingers rubbing your clit gently. I want to see your legs spread while this bullet brings you to the brink of orgasm. Them I want to bury my face in your pussy and let my tongue finish you off."

"Oh," I said breathlessly, every inch of my body on high alert.

"So if you want to do that tonight, just let me know." He grinned and stepped away from me.

I watched in silence as he pulled his credit card out and paid. My legs were trembling and my panties were wet. I could feel my face burning. My mind was racing and all I could think was, *What am I doing? What am I doing?* If my dad ever found out where I was, he would kill me. And then he'd kill Jaxon. I could barely still believe I was still here. I'd lost my mind. Absolutely lost my mind.

"Ready?" Jaxon interrupted my thoughts and grabbed his bag.

I nodded. "I'm ready," I said and followed him outside of the store. I stared at all the doors before I exited, and he smiled at me.

"Don't worry, Nancy. I'll bring you back soon. We'll go into one of the rooms when I think you're ready."

My stomach flipped at his words, and I tried not to feel excited.

***

The rest of the day seemed to pass quickly. I didn't see the other girls, and Jaxon went over body language signs with me. Lean into him if you're interested, lightly touch his arm, play with your hair, smile coyly, push your breasts out, show some cleavage, show some leg, walk with an attitude, and swing your hips. He lectured me over and over. I tried not to roll my eyes too many times, but I wasn't sure how I'd be able to do all those things without looking like a fool.

"I'm going to take you to dinner and then we'll go back to my room," he told me at the end of the lesson. "Then you can play out your fantasy."

"It's not—"

"I know. It's not your fantasy." He cut me off. "Remember what I told you, Nancy. Own your sexuality. Own your desires. It's sexier."

"Whatever." I looked away from him.

"Get ready by seven." He grinned. "I'll come and get you in your room."

"Okay." I nodded slightly.

"Don't be scared. We won't do anything you don't want to do." He reached over and caressed my cheek, touching my lips before he turned away. "I'll see you at seven."

"Okay." I squeaked out. Then I ran to my room and fell to my bed.

My heart was racing and my face was burning. I'd never felt so on edge before. The only problem was that I didn't know how high up my ledge was and I didn't know if I was going to fall. I closed my eyes and gripped the sheets as I lay there. I didn't know what was going to happen, but I knew my life was about to change.

CHAPTER FIVE

"Dinner was good. Thanks." I made small talk as we walked back to his car.

"Glad you enjoyed it. You didn't eat much."

"I wasn't that hungry," I lied. I didn't want to tell him that I'd been too busy wondering what was going to happen tonight.

"That's a shame." He opened the door for me, and I got in. "I was hoping you'd eat a lot."

"Why?" I asked him curiously.

"So you'd have energy for tonight.

"What's going to happen tonight?"

"Whatever you want," he said softly and then turned on the radio. We drove in silence until we got back to the house. "Go and get your outfit and I'll wait for you here. Then we can go to my room."

"Okay." I nodded and walked up the stairs stiffly.

I walked into the bedroom and quickly changed into the little dress. I stared at myself in the mirror and gasped. The material was completely sheer. I could see every part of my body, and my nipples were hard and clear as day. I stood there for a moment, unsure of what I should do. I felt uncomfortable going to Jaxon's room dressed like this.

But then I remembered what he'd said. If I wasn't even comfortable in my own sexuality, how was I going to get anyone? I didn't have to be ashamed of anything. So what if I was practically naked? My goal was to turn him on.

I grabbed my dressing gown and pulled it over my outfit. I'd wait to see the full effect of my outfit on him once I was in his room. I wanted to see the look in his eyes as I pulled the dressing gown off.

I hurried back down the stairs, and he looked up at me with one eyebrow raised.

"Nice outfit." He smirked, and I sweetly smiled at him.

"Well, you know, I'm going for the grandma-stripper look."

"I see." He laughed. "Let's see what you got, Grandma."

He grabbed my hand and we walked back up the stairs, heading in the direction opposite from my room. We rounded a corner and then he opened the door. I stepped into his room and gasped. It was huge, with a king-sized bed directly in the middle next to the wall. There were about twenty candles twinkling, and there was a comfortable-looking armchair to the right of the bed.

"Come." He closed the door, and I watched as he locked it with a key.

"When did you light the candles?" I asked curiously.

"A man never tells his secrets." He removed his tie and sat on the bed.

I stood in front of him and waited for him to tell me what to do. I stood there for about five minutes before I realized that he wasn't going to say anything. He was testing me. I knew it instinctively. He wanted to see what I was going to do. I bit my lower lip as I stared at him. He was leaning back in the bed and staring at me with hawk eyes.

"Do you have any music?" I said finally, straightening my shoulders. I'd show him.

"Music?" He cocked his head.

"Angel needs her music." I gave him my most seductive smile. "I don't do dances without music."

"I see." He smiled slowly. "What music do you want, Angel?"

"Surprise me." I shook out my hair as I tried to get into the role.

I watched him stand up and walk over to the corner of the room. It was then that I dropped the dressing gown. I watched him open a drawer and press a few buttons, and then I heard John

Legend playing through the speakers in his room. He turned around then, about to say something, but he froze. He stared at me for a few seconds with an intense look on his face. His eyes fell from my face and went all the way down my body and back up again. I saw a flash of desire in his expression, and his eyes looked stunned as he looked me back in the eyes again. I waited for him to say something, but all he did was smile and walk back into the bed.

I walked over to him and smiled. "Would you like a dance, sir?"

He looked up at me and nodded, and I stood there for a few seconds, unsure of what to do.

"Then come with me." I grabbed his arm, pulled him up, and brought him to the chair.

I pushed him down and turned away from him. I was about to start dancing, but my body wouldn't move. I stood there for a few minutes and tried to think. *What's holding you back, Nancy? Do you want to be here? Do you want to do this?* I knew in that moment that I did want to do this.

I closed my eyes and tried to imagine what I wanted to happen. I could see myself gyrating on his lap. I could feel his hands reaching around to grab my breasts. I'd turn around and face him and he'd reach down and take his breasts in my mouth. He'd grab my ass, and I'd feel his hardness between my legs.

My eyes popped open and I swallowed hard as I realized that I was incredibly turned on. I started moving my hips back and forth and danced to the music, allowing it to let me lose myself. I pretended I was at a nightclub, on the dance floor with friends, just letting go. I moved backwards and lowered myself onto Jaxon's lap, slowly gyrating on him as I ran my hands through his hair. I could feel his cock hardening beneath me as I rubbed my ass up and down on his lap.

I leaned back into his chest and rest my head against his neck. I could feel his breath next to my ear. I increased my pace, wanting to make him harder, and I could feel his heart beating as I moved. I waited for him to touch me, but he didn't. I started to feel frustrated. I wanted him to touch me. I increased my pace and felt his body stiffening, but still, he did nothing.

I jumped up and turned around to face him, lowering myself onto his lap again. I stared into his eyes as I moved to the music, but he was giving nothing away. I pushed my breasts against his chest as I moved and ran my hands down his shirt, losing myself in the music and moment. My fingers deftly undid his shirt until it was wide open, but still, he didn't touch me.

I ran my fingernails down his chest and increased my pace. This time, I felt the hardness in his pants directly between my legs and I rubbed myself back and forth on him. I could feel myself growing wetter and wetter. I needed him to touch me, but he did nothing. Finally, I grabbed his hands, pulled them around me, and placed them on my ass.

"You can touch me, you know," I whispered to him, and he smiled.

His fingers moved swiftly, and I felt him pull my negligee completely up so that my ass was completely uncovered. His fingers squeezed my ass as I moved, and he pushed me down on his hardness as I moved back and forth. I closed my eyes as his fingers caressed my skin and I moved back and forth on him. I pulled back slightly, lifted my arms up, and pulled the negligee off completely so that I was naked besides the thong. I saw his eyes narrowed and felt his sharp intake of breath. He hadn't expected that.

I smiled to myself as I pushed my breasts against his naked chest. His hands ran up and down my back, and I groaned as my panties grew heavier and heavier. I reached down, unbuckled his pants, and jumped off his lap. I pulled his pants off and threw them on the ground. He was wearing a pair of white boxers, and I climbed back onto his lap and started dancing again. His cock felt harder and closer to me. I felt like I was fucking him even though we had material between us stopping that from happening.

I pushed myself up slightly and brushed my breasts across his face. He lightly licked my nipple as they brushed past his lips. I moaned and moved faster. I grabbed his hands and put them on my breasts, wanting to feel him touching me. He obliged and played with my nipples lightly before pinching them. I increased the pace of my movements and reached down to adjust his cock between my legs. I was so close to coming. I could feel it. It was then that he pushed me off of him and stood up.

"Uh uh," he whispered, his eyes narrowing. "You can't come."

"What?" I looked at him with lust-filled eyes.

"You're not doing this for you. You're playing a role. You're not Angel. You are Nancy. When I know you can do this as Nancy, then you can come."

"What?" I groaned as I stood there staring at him. His hardness was bulging in his pants, and I could still remember the feel of it between my legs.

"You need to let go, Nancy. A man wants the real you. Not the illusion of you. Not a character you put on. I need you to be you."

"What?" I moaned, feeling frustrated.

"Get on the bed," he commanded me, and I got on it quickly, anxious for a release.

He walked over to the corner again and grabbed something from a drawer. He walked back with a pair of handcuffs and a feather.

"What are you doing?" I stared at him curiously, my heart still racing.

"Lie back." He kneeled on the bed and pushed me back. He grabbed my wrists and handcuffed each one to the bedpost behind me. He ran his fingers across my breasts and down to my thong, which he promptly pulled off. "Spread your legs," he commanded me, and I slowly opened my legs. His gaze darkened as he smiled.

He reached down and I felt his lips pressing against mine. He softly lowered his body onto mine, and I felt his chest crushing my breasts, his cock nestled between my legs.

"Oh," I moaned and closed my eyes as he kissed down my neck and moved back and forth gently. I tried to reach out to touch him, but I couldn't move my arms. His tongue licked a trail along my neck and collarbone, and then he stood back up. "I want to make you mine." His voice was low and hoarse, and I shivered in the darkness.

I felt the light touch of the feather being guided along my naked body, and I knew that I needed to become his as well. I wanted to become his. I had to become his. I whimpered slightly as I felt something cold touch my skin.

"I'm going to make you forget your own name." His voice became louder as he guided the feather farther down.

"Please," I whispered as I felt what must have been an ice cube grazing my nipple. "Oh." I trembled as he ran the melting ice cube across my breasts. I could feel the residue of water on my skin.

"Please what, Nancy?"

"Please," I moaned in high anticipation.

It was then that I felt his warm breath on my breasts as he eagerly licked up the water, sucking gently on my nipples as if he were enjoying every last drop of water. I felt the tip of the feather moving between my legs as he teased me. I gasped as his finger accidentally grazed my clit, and I cried out when his finger touched me again. That hadn't been an accident.

His finger gently rubbed me, and I closed my eyes as I realized that my climax was building up again. Then his finger slowly entered my. I gasped as I felt him inside me. My body started trembling and I felt like I was going to burst, but something inside me was unwilling to let go. His finger left me quickly, and I opened my eyes in dismay, blinking up at him in confusion.

"Why did you stop?" I whispered.

"I'm going to leave you now," he said.

I heard him step away from me, and I froze. My hands were still handcuffed to the bed and I couldn't move.

"What do you mean?" I cried out, my whole body aching for him.

"You're not ready yet."

"I am," I whispered, embarrassed to admit it.

"No, no you're not." His fingers trailed between my legs again and he played with my wetness. "Your body is ready, but you are not."

There was silence in the room as he continued playing with me. I clenched my legs to trap his fingers. I needed him to know how badly I wanted him.

"That's not enough, Nancy." His voice was deep, and I could imagine the look on his face. "I will not make you mine until every fiber in your body has to have me."

"I do want you," I whispered.

"Not enough. I will not take you until you are screaming out my name and begging me. I won't take you—not until there is no other thought in your mind but me inside you. I won't take you—not until I know I possess every inch of you." He leaned down and pressed his lips gently against mine, and then he walked away.

"I'm ready!" I called out, in need of a release. "Please."

"You're not relaxing enough. I will not bring you to orgasm until you can relax. That is lesson one."

"Please!" I cried out, needing to feel his hands against me again.

"You don't want it badly enough. You need to want it with every fiber of your being. You need to crave an orgasm so much that you can't even think straight. You need to want it so badly that your mind doesn't control your body. You need to want it so much that you can't even see past your desire or need." He paused. "That's step one, Nancy. Once you can lose yourself in the moment, once you have lost all those inhibitions, then we can start again and you can experience the climax of your life."

"Jaxon," I called after him.

"Yes, Nancy?" He stopped and looked back at me. His eyes were dark and his face was unsmiling.

"Can you untie me from the bed please?" I whispered and bit down on my lip. I wanted to ask him to do more, but I didn't know what to say.

"If I untie you, this lesson is over. You know that, right?" His voice sounded hoarse.

"Yes, I know." I trembled on the bed. "I know."

"Fine." He walked over to me and gentled undid the handcuffs. "Here." He picked up my negligee and handed it to me. "Put this on and go back to your room."

"So we're done for the night?" I asked softly, quickly putting my clothes back on.

"We're done." He nodded and then his lips curled up. "This is a lovers' academy, Nancy. I'm here to teach you about sex. I'm not here to whisper sweet nothings to you in the middle of the night."

"I know that." I glared at him and headed to the door. "I wasn't expecting that."

"When you trust me enough to go all the way with a lesson, let me know." He turned away from me, and I walked out of the door in silence.

***

I left my room after about two hours and walked around the corner, heading to Jaxon's room. I wanted to tell him that I trusted him and wanted to continue with the lesson. I figured that maybe it wasn't such a bad idea. It would be good to become a master of seduction if I was going to get Hunter. It had nothing to do with the fact that I wanted Jaxon. Nothing at all. I just wanted to come. I needed him to bring me to orgasm. I could think of nothing else.

I was also surprised at just how much I had let go with him. I'd been someone else. Someone I hadn't recognized. When I had danced on his lap, I'd felt alive. His cock growing beneath me had made me powerful. If I were honest, I'd admit that I wanted more than just a simple orgasm. I'd wanted to ride him. I'd wanted to take him inside me. I wanted more than just to get off. I wanted him to get off as well.

I tried to ignore the thoughts in my mind that were whispering Hunter's name. I had no idea what he was doing with Shannon. I had no idea if they were already fucking. She certainly owed me no loyalties. And if I were honest with myself, I'd admit that it didn't seem like he even remembered me—unless he was faking it for some reason.

I wanted to continue on with Jaxon's lessons. I wanted to own my body, own my sexuality. I wanted to be taught by the master. And a part of me wanted to see if I could figure him out. I walked swiftly, my legs trembling slightly as I realized what I was about to commit to. There would be no going back once I went back to his room.

I was just about to turn the corner when my body stiffened. I heard his voice before I saw him.

"So, Jaxon, how's it going?" a man spoke in a low voice.

"I'm working on it, Dad." His voice sounded annoyed.

Dad? I stopped in surprise. His dad was here? I was about to turn around when I heard Jaxon's dad speaking again.

"She seemed like she'd be easy on the train."

I froze as I recognized the voice. Was Jaxon's dad the man that had been sitting across from me on the train? I slowly peeked around the corner and stared at the two men as they stood there talking. Jaxon's face looked angry. And his father? His father was definitely the man from the train.

"Dad." His voice was terse. "I can't talk about this right now. There's been a complication."

"Remember the plan," his dad said softly. "Just remember the plan."

"It's all going according to plan. Just trust me." Jaxon's voice was tight and his face turned into a grimace. "She's like putty in my hands."

I stood there in shock and leaned back against the wall. Was he talking about me? Why hadn't he been sitting with his dad on the train?

"I don't care if she's like fucking glue, Jaxon. Just remember the plan."

"I remember, Dad." Jaxon's voice was terse. "Don't worry. She'll be in my bed before you know it."

"And once she is, we move to stage two." The older man laughed. "And then, Nancy won't know what hit her."

"That's right," Jaxon responded. "She'll be well and truly under my spell then."

AUTHOR'S NOTE

The Love Trials Part II and The Love Trials Part III are available.

Please join my mailing list to be notified as soon as the second book is out: http://jscooperauthor.com/mail-list.

Thank you for reading and purchasing this book. I love to hear from readers so feel free to send me an email at jscooperauthor@gmail.com at any time.

You can also join me on my Facebook page: https://www.facebook.com/J.S.Cooperauthor.

LIST OF AVAILABLE J. S. COOPER BOOKS

You can see a list of all my books on my website: https://www.facebook.com/J.S.Cooperauthor.

The Forever Love Boxed Set (Books 1-3)

Crazy Beautiful Love

The Ex Games

The Private Club

After The Ex Games

Everlasting Sin

Scarred

Healed

The Last Boyfriend

The Last Husband

Before Lucky

The Other Side of Love

Zane & Lucky's First Christmas

LIST OF BOOKS AVAILABLE
FOR PREORDER

ILLUSION

The day started like every other day...

Bianca London finds herself kidnapped and locked up in a van with a strange man. Ten hours later, they're dumped on a deserted island. Bianca has no idea what's going on and her attraction to this stranger is the only thing keeping her fear at bay.

Jakob Bradley wants only to figure out why they've been left on the island and how they can get off. But as the days go by, he can't ignore his growing fascination with Bianca.

In order to survive, Bianca and Jakob must figure out how they're connected, but as they grow closer, secrets are revealed that may destroy everything they thought they knew about each other.

TAMING MY PRINCE CHARMING

When Lola met Xavier, Prince of Romerius, she was immediately attracted to his dark, handsome good looks and sparkling green eyes. She spent a whirlwind weekend with him and almost fell for his charm, until he humiliated her and she fled.

Lola wasn't prepared to find out that Xavier was her new professor and her new boss. She also wasn't prepared for the sparks that flew every time they were together. When Xavier takes her on a work trip, she is shocked when they are mobbed by the paparazzi and agrees to go to Romerius with Xavier to pretend she is his fiancé.

Only Lola had no idea that Xavier had a master plan from the moment he met her. He wanted a week to make her his, so that he could get her out of his system. Only Xavier had no idea that fate had another plan for him.

GUARDING HIS HEART

Leonardo Maxwell was shocked when his best friend, Zane Beaumont fell in love and got married. While he is happy for his friend, he knows that he definitely doesn't want to go the love and marriage route. He knows that there is nothing that can come from either of the two.

When his father calls him and tells him that it's time for him to take over the family business, he does so reluctantly. He's never liked the attention he gets as a billionaire's son, but he knows it's his duty.

Leo is not prepared for the animosity that he gets from his new assistant, Hannah on his first day of work. He has no idea why she hates him, but he's glad for it. He doesn't have time to waste staring at her beautiful long legs or her pink luscious lips. As far as he's concerned they can have a strictly professional relationship. However, that all changes when they go on their first work trip together.

IF ONLY ONCE (THE MARTELLI BROTHERS)

It's the quiet ones that can surprise you

Vincent Martelli grew up as the quiet one in his family. While his brothers got into trouble, he tried to take the studious route, even though he always found himself caught up in their mess.

When Vincent is paired up with a no-nonsense girl in one of his classes, he is frustrated and annoyed. Katia is everything he doesn't want in a woman and yet, he can't seem to get her out of his mind.

Then Katia shows up at his house with his brother's girlfriend, Maddie and he finds himself offering her his bed, when her car breaks down. When Katia accepts he is shocked, but he vows to himself that he won't let down his walls. As far as he is concerned there is no way that he could date someone like her. Only life never does seem to go as planned, does it?

REDEMPTION

One fight can change everything

Hudson Blake has two weeks to get his best friend Luke ready for the fight of his life. If Luke wins the championship he will receive one million dollars to help out the family of the woman he loved and lost.

Hudson's girlfriend, Riley doesn't want Hudson or Luke to fight and so she enlists the help of her best friend, Eden. However, Riley didn't count on Eden finding a battered and bruised Luke sexy and charismatic.

Luke has never felt as alive as he does practicing for the championship. He has vowed that he is not going to let anything get in his way. He knows that he is fighting for redemption and love. And he can't afford to lose.

THE ONLY WAY

Jared Martelli is the youngest Martelli brother, but he's also the most handsome and most confident. There is nothing that gets in the way of what he wants and he has no time for love.

Jared blows off college to start his own business and it's his goal to make a million dollars within five years. He's happy working hard and playing the field. That is until he meets Pippa one night at a bar. Pippa is headstrong, beautiful and has absolutely no interest in him. And that's one thing Jared can't accept.

He decides to pursue Pippa with plans of dropping her once she submits to his charms. Only his plans go awry when he realizes that Pippa has plans of her own and they don't include him.

TO YOU, FROM ME

Sometimes the greatest gifts in life come when you least expect them

Zane Beaumont never expected to fall in love with Lucky Morgan. He never expected to have a household full of children. He never knew that his life could be so full of laughter and love.

To You, From Me chronicles Zane and Lucky's relationship from the good times to the bad. It shows why marriage can be the best and worst experience in your life. Experience the gamut of emotions that Zane goes through as he goes through the journey of being a husband and father.

CRAZY BEAUTIFUL CHRISTMAS

Logan, Vincent and Jared Martelli decide to spend Christmas together with the women they love. Only none of their plans are going right. When they find a pregnancy test all three of them start to panic about becoming a father. Only they don't know which one of them is the daddy to be.

Join the Martelli Brothers on their quest for the perfect Christmas holiday. They may have a few more bumps in the road than they planned, but ultimately it will be the season of giving and loving.

ABOUT THE AUTHOR

J. S. Cooper was born in London, England and moved to Florida her last year of high school. After completing law school at the University of Iowa (from the sunshine to cold) she moved to Los Angeles to work for a Literacy non profit as an Americorp Vista. She then moved to New York to study the History of Education at Columbia University and took a job at a workers rights non profit upon graduation.

She enjoys long walks on the beach (or short), hot musicians, dogs, reading (duh) and lots of drama filled TV Shows.

Printed in Great Britain
by Amazon